bat

fish

dragon

alien

backhoe

human

Gilles Bachelet has been creating picture books since 2002 and currently teaches illustration at the School of Art in Cambrai, France. His previous books include *Mrs. White Rabbit* (Eerdmans) as well as *My Cat, the Silliest Cat in the World* and *When the Silliest Cat Was Small* (both Abrams).

First published in the United States in 2019 by
Eerdmans Books for Young Readers,
an imprint of Wm. B. Eerdmans Publishing Co.
4035 Park East Court, Grand Rapids, Michigan 49546
www.eerdmans.com/youngreaders

Originally published in France under the title *Une histoire qui . . .*
© 2016 Éditions du Seuil
English-language translation © 2019 Eerdmans Books for Young Readers

Manufactured in China

27 26 25 24 23 22 21 20 19   1 2 3 4 5 6 7 8 9

Library of Congress Cataloging-in-Publication Data

Names: Bachelet, Gilles, author, illustrator.
Title: A story that grows / written and illustrated by Gilles Bachelet.
Other titles: Une histoire qui.... English
Description: Grand Rapids MI : Eerdmans Books for Young Readers, 2019. |
    Summary: Illustrations and easy-to-read text demonstrate that bedtime
    stories are as unique as the parents and children who share them.
Identifiers: LCCN 2018025859 | ISBN 9780802855121
Subjects: | CYAC: Books and reading—Fiction. | Parent and child—Fiction. |
    Bedtime—Fiction.
Classification: LCC PZ7.B13213 Sto 2019 | DDC [E]—dc23 LC record available at
https://lccn.loc.gov/2018025859

A Story That Grows

Gilles Bachelet

Eerdmans Books for Young Readers

Grand Rapids, Michigan

A very gentle mom,
a chubby-cheeked child,
a cuddly friend with whiskers . . .

. . . a story that grows.

A dad with whiskers,
a cozy warm child,
a friend with a long beak . . .

. . . a story
that's
made
to
melt.

A mom with a long beak,
a child perched up high,
a cuddly friend that's all neck . . .

. . . a story that soars . . . .

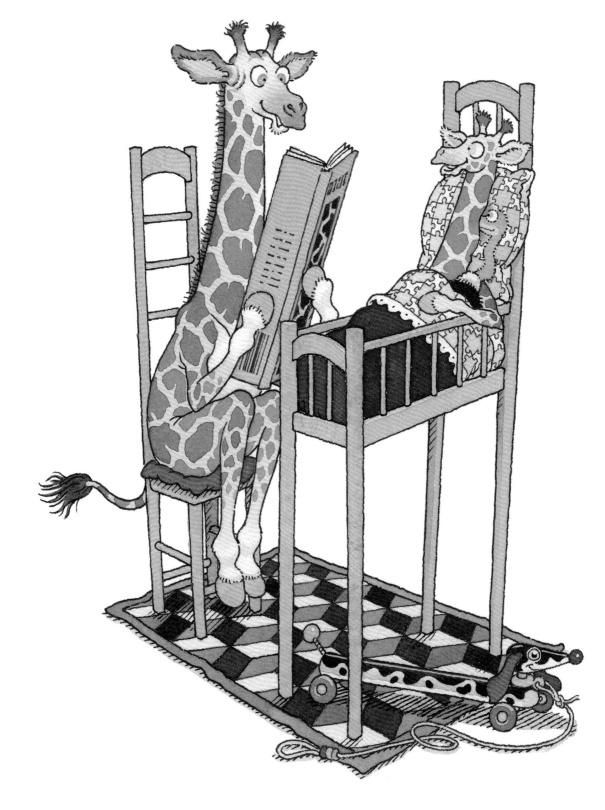

A dad who's all neck,
a child with patchwork patterns,
a friend that hides its head . . .

lasts.

that

story

. . . a

A mom who hides her head,
a child tucked under the covers,
a cuddly friend with a spiral shell . . .

. . . a story that hatches.

A dad with a spiral shell,
a child who smiles,
a cuddly friend that hangs upside down . . .

. . . a story . . . . . . that . . . . . . takes . . . . . its . . . . . time . . . .

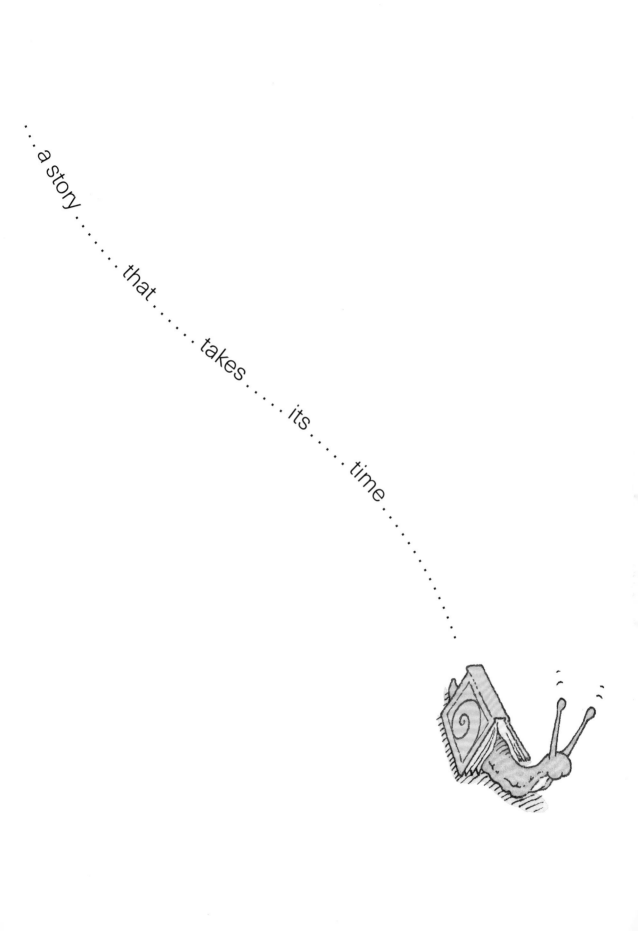

A mom who hangs upside down,
a child with her head in the clouds,
a friend that's ready for a swim . . .

. . . a story

that turns

topsy-turvy.

A dad who's ready for a swim,
a child who splashes around,
a friend that breathes smoke . . .

. . . a story that ripples . . . . .

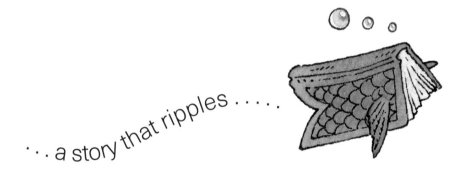

A mom who breathes smoke,
a child tucked in his cave,
a cuddly friend from outer space . . .

...a story that sparkles.

A dad from outer space,
a child who chatters,
a mechanical friend . . .

...a ....
story ....
that ....
flies ....
by ....

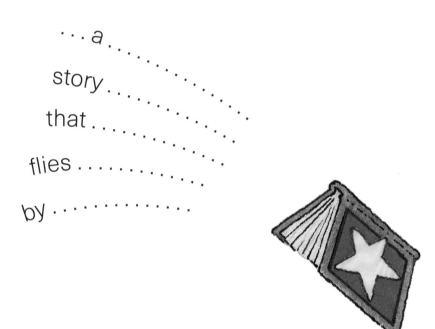

A mechanical mother,
a child full of smiles,
a friend that stretches . . .

 . . . a
story
that
protects.

A dad who stretches,
a child snuggled in for the night,
a cuddly friend that comforts . . .

. . . a story that is off to sleep.

panda

walrus

stork

giraffe

ostrich

snail